KATHERINE
AND THE GARBAGE DUMP

by

Martha Morris

Illustrated by

Yvonne Cathcart

SECOND STORY Press

KATHERINE LOVED HER BACKYARD. It was big and beautiful. And right in the middle stood a tall willow tree, with Katherine's sandbox underneath. Katharine was just adding a flag to her new sandtower when a juice can zinged over the fence and crashed into the sandbox.

"Hey!" said Katherine.

Her neighbour, Mr. Jenkin, popped his head above the fence.
"Oh dear – so sorry. Never thought it would hit your sandbox. I'll pick it up later – terrible hurry. Got to go. Bye."

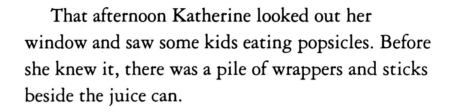

That afternoon Katherine looked out her window and saw some kids eating popsicles. Before she knew it, there was a pile of wrappers and sticks beside the juice can.

Later that evening Katherine peered out her window again. There beside the pile were two coffee cups and some yucky newspapers.

Katherine sighed. "I'll clean it all up tomorrow," she said.

The next morning, Katherine was woken up by a crashing and a banging and a screeching. She looked out the window. A truck was dumping garbage into her backyard!

Katherine ran outside.

"Hey!" said Katherine to the truck driver. "Do you think this is a garbage dump or something?"

The truck driver nodded his head. "Yep, the Chief told me to take this garbage to the new dump. I saw all this junk just lying around, so I knew this must be it. I got orders to dump the garbage, and that is what I did. Talk to the Chief."

And the truck driver drove away.

"You've got it all wrong," said Katherine.

In a flash Katherine put on her rubber boots and walked down to the City Garbage Department. Just inside the building she saw a desk.

"Yes, dear?" said the person sitting behind it.

"I would like to talk to the Chief of Garbage, please, if I may," said Katherine.

"Well, I don't know. She is a very busy person," said the secretary. "We will have to see."

"Well just for a minute," the Chief chimed in. "What can I do for you, sweetie?"

"Excuse me, Ms. Chief, but a truck dumped garbage in my backyard this morning."

"Oh? Are you ever lucky. How come *you* get to have your very own garbage dump?" asked the Chief. "Are you the Superchief's kid or something?"

"I don't *want* the garbage," said Katherine. "You've got it all wrong." And she stomped off home.

By now, *everyone* seemed to think Katherine's backyard was a garbage dump. The garbage pile was growing huge.

Katherine picked up the phone and said, "I would like to talk to the Superchief of Garbage, please if I may."

"Well, I don't know. He is a very busy person," said the secretary. "We will have to see."

"Well, just for a minute," said the Superchief of Garbage, picking up his phone. "What can I do for you, honey?"

"Excuse me, Superchief, but a truck has dumped garbage in my backyard and it's all over the place."

"I see, I see. But then your backyard must be a garbage dump."

"You've got it all wrong," said Katherine.

"The truck driver had his orders. Anyway, dear, it is not *my* garbage. Talk to the Head Keeper of the Keep Our City Clean Committee."

"Wait a minute," said Katherine.

But he had already hung up.

Katherine tried to look out her window to see what was happening, but there was garbage everywhere! She closed all the windows, put on her baseball cap and climbed up onto her roof.

Garbage was piled almost as high as the top of the willow tree. It was spilling over the fence and into Mr. Jenkin's backyard. There were big bottles, cartons of cans, mountains of newspapers, smelly shoes, plastic plates, mushy melons and sticky, stinky stuff all over the place.

Another dumptruck came. The garbage grew and spilled into the street. People walking by held their noses and said things like "P-e-e-e-w" and "Don't they have a Recycling Box?" and "Yuck!"

Another dumptruck came. The garbage grew so high and so wide that cars were stuck on the street. Now even television reporters in helicopters flew over the dump. There were TV cameras whirring, car drivers shouting and police officers scratching their heads.

"Enough," said Katherine, "is enough." She jumped off the roof, climbed over the garbage and headed down Main Street. She marched straight into City Hall.

There were the Chief of Garbage, the Superchief of Garbage and the secretaries. And there, sitting in a big, red chair, was the Head Keeper of the Keep Our City Clean Committee.

Katherine walked right up to the Head Keeper, took off her baseball cap and said, "I would like to talk to you Mr. Head Keeper, please if I may."

The Head Keeper said, "Yes dear. Stand up then."

"I am standing, Sir," said Katherine.

"Oh well, I see you are a kid. We are very busy people, dear. There seems to be a national emergency. Something about garbage."

"Yes," said Katherine. "They are dumping garbage in my backyard."

"Who is?" said the Head Keeper.

"Not me," said the Chief of Garbage.

"It's not *my* garbage," said the Superchief of Garbage.

"It is all your fault we're in this mess," said Mr.
Head Keeper and pointed his finger at Katherine.

Katherine opened her mouth wide.

How she wanted to sink her teeth into that
finger!

Katherine stood up on the big red chair.
"You've *all* got it all wrong!" she yelled at the top
of her lungs.

Katherine put her baseball cap back on.
She marched out of City Hall, up Main Street,
over the garbage and up onto her roof.

"Excuse me," she said to the people below.
"I would like to talk to you, please if I may."

"I," said Katherine, "am going to clean up
my backyard."

People cheered. They got out of their cars and
stood around Katherine and clapped.

Katherine pulled up her rubber boots,
pulled down her baseball cap, and started.
She made special piles for things to be recycled.

"And here," said Katherine, "is the perfect
spot for compost. The garden will love it."

When the people saw what she was doing, they began to help. The TV reporters gathered bottles to take to the store. The truck drivers got out of the dumptrucks and collected plastic things that could be used again. "Hey, look at this," hollered one of them as he showed off the thing-a-ma-jig he was making. Even Mr. Jenkin helped by putting the cans in a recycling box.

And no one stopped until the juice can right at the very bottom of the pile was picked up.

How wonderful the yard looked! And all the people were having a great time making spectacular thing-a-ma-jigs. When it was all done, Katherine shook each and every one's hand.

And so it wasn't at all surprising

when Katherine was made Mayor

of the whole city

very soon afterwards.